polar bear

created by Trevor Ricketts and Christopher O'Hare

A Random House PICTUREBACK® Book

Random House 🏠 New York

Copyright © 2000 by Collingwood O'Hare Entertainment Ltd. All rights reserved under International and Pan-American Copyright Conventions. Published in the United States by Random House, Inc., New York, and simultaneously in Canada by Random House of Canada Limited, Toronto. Originally published in slightly different form by HarperCollins Publishers Ltd, London, in 2000.

www.randomhouse.com/kids

Library of Congress Control Number: 2001087885

ISBN 0-375-81377-2

First American Edition
Printed in the United States of America   November 2001
10 9 8 7 6 5 4 3 2 1

There is a bear

Who lives up north.

A polar bear

He is, of course.

But don't believe

All you are told,

Because this bear

Just hates the cold!

He dreamed one day

Of running away.

He'd sail a boat

To Saint-Tropez.

He'd cross the sea,

Way past the ice,

Toward the sun,

To somewhere nice.

He'd find a beach
And build a hut.
Eat fresh fruit
And coconut.

He sighed and said,

"That would be fun.

But I'm stuck here,

Where there is no sun.

I feel so cold.

It's just not fair.

How can I be

A polar bear?"

The days went by

And Bear got sadder.

More snow came down,

Which made him madder.

So he packed a bag

And put on his coat.

He was leaving home

For the nearest boat.

He trudged away,

Through snow quite thick,

Past icicles

Too big to lick.

Of home, sweet home,

He began to think.

That he missed his mom

Made his heart sink.

His face went numb.

His fingers froze.

He lost all sense

In his little toes.

He kept on going

But got nowhere,

A tired and frozen

Little polar bear.

But wait a sec!

What's that ahead?

A tiny house

With a roof of red.

When he got closer,

He began to realize

The house was his.

Oh! What a surprise!

He opened the door—

His mommy was there.

Smiling, she said,

"You're a funny young bear.

I watched you walk

For an hour or more.

You meant to travel

Far, I'm sure."

outside,

ere in the snow

re little footprints

In a circular row.

The little bear looked—

His mommy was right.

He had to laugh.

It was the funniest sight.

"Come on," she said,

And gave him a hug.

"Here's a hot drink

In your favorite mug."

Later they had

Some honey and bread.

She gave him a bath

And took him to bed.

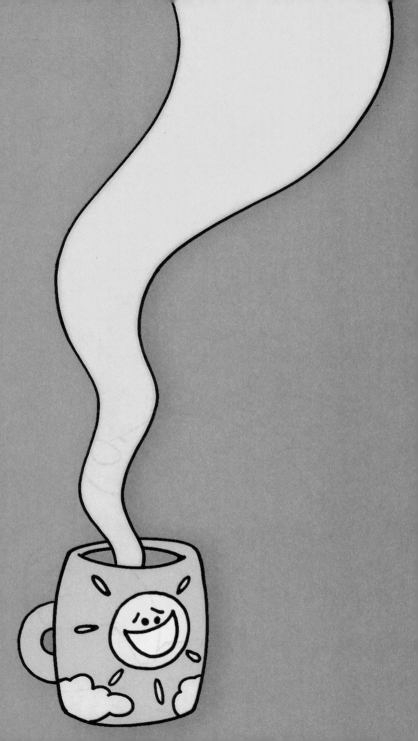

After a story,

Off went the light.

And closing the door,

She said, "Good night."

The little bear smiled

As he lay in bed.

Thoughts of the cold

Were out of his head.

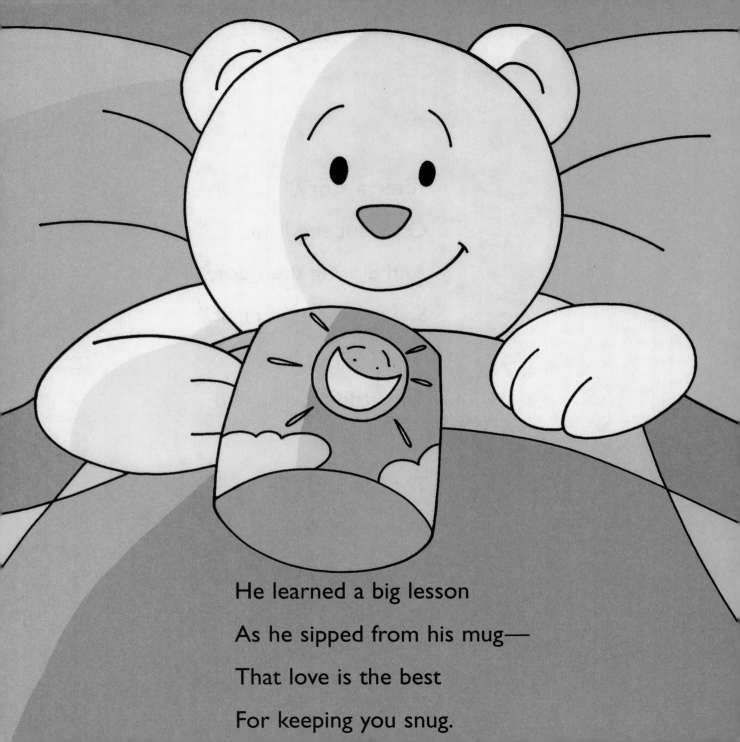

He learned a big lesson

As he sipped from his mug—

That love is the best

For keeping you snug.